Noah's Park

DREAMER HAS A NIGHTMARE

Written by Richard Hays
Illustrated by Chris Sharp

Faith Kids

an imprint of Cook Communications, Colorado Springs, Colorado 80918
Cook Communications, Paris, Ontario
Kingsway Communications, Eastbourne, England

DREAMER HAS A NIGHTMARE
©1999 by The Illustrated Word, Inc.

First printing, 1999
Printed in Canada
03 02 01 00   5 4 3 2

Digital art and design: Gary Currant
Executive Producer: Kenneth R. Wilcox

Library of Congress Cataloging-in-Publication Data

Hays, Richard.
    Dreamer Has a Nightmare / written by Richard Hays ; Illustrated by Chris Sharp.
       p. cm. -- (Noah's Park)
    Summary: After Dreamer the rhinoceros tells the other animals about his nightmare, they
cannot sleep either, until Ponder the frog helps them to realize that God will keep them safe.
    ISBN 0-7814-3368-1
    [1. Animal Fiction. 2. Nightmare Fiction. 3. Noah (Biblical figure) Fiction. 4. Christian life
Fiction.] I. Sharp, Chris, 1954- ill. II. Title. III. Series: Hays, Richard. Noah's Park.
PZ7.H314924Dr 1999
[E]--dc21
                                                  99-39082
                                                    CIP

Faith Parenting Guide

Dreamer Has a Nightmare

Trust: I want to help my child learn to rely on God in the everyday situations of life.

Sound: Read the story of *Dreamer Has a Nightmare*. Talk about nightmares that you or your child have had. Discuss how the nightmare made you feel and what you did to try to feel better about it. Did the nightmare come from any real-life experience?

Sight: Look at the fun pictures in the story that show the ways that Dreamer and the other animals tried to stay awake. Have you ever tried to keep yourself from falling asleep? What do you do when you feel afraid? God says that you can come to Him for comfort and He will protect you. Proverbs 1:33 tells us, "Whoever listens to me will live in safety and be at ease, without fear of harm."

Touch: Say a prayer together to help your child feel God is near even when you are asleep. Say something like this: "Dear God, please be with us through the night. Bless us with good dreams and watch over us. Help us to know that You are always with us. Amen." Make a little dream book and write down some of your child's dreams. Find a Bible verse that will help your child feel God's love and protection and write it in the dream book.

Dreamer the rhinoceros waddled over to the pond and looked deeply into the water. He saw several shiny fish swimming lazily back and forth. As he watched, his large head swayed from side to side, following the fish.

His eyelids began to droop lower and lower. Finally, his eyes closed, and Dreamer's head dropped with a splash into the pond.

Shadow the raccoon and Screech the monkey, who were watching
Dreamer from a nearby tree, hurried over to the pond
and pulled the rhino's huge head from the water.

The raccoon climbed onto Dreamer's
head and opened one large eye.

"Amazing. He's still asleep,"
he told Screech.

"Never felt a thing,"
the monkey noted.

With a rhino-sized snort, Dreamer stood up,
causing the raccoon to slide down his nose until he
hung by one paw from the rhino's horn.
"I wasn't sleeping," Dreamer said.
"I was only resting my eyes.
How did I get so wet,
Shadow?"

The raccoon laughed and then skipped into the woods with Screech. Dreamer slowly walked over to Cozy Cave. Everyone thought he slept all the time, and maybe he did take his share of little naps and snoozes. An active rhino needs lots of rest.

In the cave, Dreamer lay
down on the cool dirt and
once again closed his eyes. *I love to sleep,*
thought the rhino, *because then I can dream.*
In my dreams, I can go anywhere
and do anything. Then when I wake up,
I'm still safe at home in Noah's Park,
right where I want to be . . .
"ZZZzzzz."

Ponder and Honk stopped at the pond for a drink. They could hear Dreamer's loud snores coming from the cave.

"He sleeps all the time," said Honk, admiring his reflection in the water. "When does he have time to bathe? He really needs to work on his appearance."

"Looks are not that important, Honk," Ponder reminded the camel. "Dreamer does sleep a lot, but he is a very smart rhinoceros. We often depend on his ideas. Remember, what's inside you is important, too, and besides, Dreamer loves to dream."

"Arrrgh!" Dreamer let out a huge roar.
Seconds later, he came galloping
out of the cave right into the pond,
taking Ponder and
Honk with him …

right
into
the
water.

"What's wrong, Dreamer?" Honk sputtered, removing a slippery fish from his ear.

"My dream! My dream! It was scary. I've never had a scary dream before. I was so afraid!" The rhinoceros stumbled out of the water and crashed, sobbing, to the ground.

Ponder hopped over to his friend. "You had a nightmare," he told him. "A nightmare is just a scary dream. It's not real."

Dreamer looked at the old frog.
"It was real, and it was awful."

All of the animals of Noah's Park gathered around the frightened rhino.

"What was so horrible, Dreamer?" Stretch the giraffe asked. "Were there scary monsters or giant bugs."

Dreamer shook his head, but did not say a word. He just huddled on the ground.

"Was this your first nightmare?" asked Ivory the elephant. "I remember mine. I dreamed that a big wind carried me away."

"It must have been a tornado," laughed Shadow, twirling around.

"In my first nightmare a giant tree tried to swallow me. I think it was a dogwood tree."

"I got stuck in a mud hole in my first nightmare," Honk said. "It was terrible. I got very dirty."

"All I remember about my first nightmare is a big paw and giant snapping teeth," shivered Screech.
"No, I think that was my sister."

"I had a nightmare where my mane kept growing until it covered my whole body," remembered Howler the lion. "I couldn't see or move because the hair was so thick. I felt like a bush."

Dreamer looked up at the others.
"It was nothing like any of those," he said.
"Mine was much scarier because it was so real!"

For the next two days Dreamer stared at the water in the pond. He did not sleep or eat.

"You need to sleep, Dreamer, and you need to eat something," Ponder told his friend on the third day. "Here, I brought you a bunch of bananas."

"Thank you, Ponder." Dreamer swallowed the bananas with a single gulp. "I did need to eat, but I'm never going to go to sleep again."

The next day Dreamer was still awake, but he had to hold his eyelids up to keep his eyes open.

Ponder again brought the rhino some food.

"You must get over this," said the wise frog. "Most animals have nightmares, but they still go to sleep the next night. Maybe you should tell us about your nightmare."

The tired rhino looked at Ponder and then nodded his head in agreement.

"We were all there. You, Shadow, and you, Stretch, and you, Howler. All of us. We were in some kind of a building that floated on the water. And the water … it was everywhere. Rain was pouring out of the sky. Huge waves were crashing all around us. It was very dark, but great bolts of lightning and thunder exploded around us."

"There was a man in the building, and he tried to keep us calm. But the water just kept pouring down. I was more afraid than ever before. I felt like the rain would never stop."

When Dreamer finished his story, most of the animals agreed that it was the scariest nightmare they had ever heard. Ponder just looked at Dreamer, though, and did not say anything.

That night all the animals slept except Dreamer. A short time later Screech came screaming out to the pond.

"I had Dreamer's nightmare!" Screech told the others. "It was so real. I'm never going to go to sleep again!"

The next evening the animals all went to
sleep again–all, that is, except for two.
This night Dreamer and Screech
stayed awake, their eyelids held open.

Sometime in the middle of the night,
there were two more screams.

"I had Dreamer's nightmare,"
sobbed Ivory.

"And I did, too," cried Howler.

"We're never going to go to
sleep again," they said together.

When the next darkness fell, there were four animals with their eyes barely open. Ponder looked at them and shook his head. But he still did not say anything. Before the night was over, Stretch, Honk, and Shadow had all had Dreamer's nightmare, too.

The following day, Ponder floated around on the far side of the pond. Finally, as the sun set, he went back to the cave where nearly all of the animals were huddled, each doing his best to keep his eyes open and to stay awake.

"The nightmare you have been having is not a nightmare at all," started the frog, as he paced in front of his friends. "You are remembering something that happened to all of us a long time ago.

"The building you are dreaming about was actually an ark, a type of boat. God told Noah to build the ark and then gather some of each type of animal onto it. When Noah had done this, it began to rain. It rained for forty days and forty nights. The rain caused the great Flood that you are dreaming about. You were all on the ark. You were just too young or too frightened to remember.

"I was on the ark, too, but I watched and listened to Noah during the storm. Noah knew that God was with us all the time. He knew that God would protect us and keep us safe. So each time that Noah became afraid, he would remember that God was with him. God gave Noah the strength to be brave.

"Now, you can be brave, too, by understanding that God is always with you. You can go to sleep knowing that God will protect you."

"I think I can be brave," said Dreamer slowly, "if I know God is with me."

"Me, too," agreed Screech. "I can be strong with God's help."

"Me, too." "Me, too!" chimed in the others.

That night all of the animals slept soundly. There were no more nightmares, or, if there were, the animals were brave because they knew that God was with them all the time.

Dreamer again enjoyed his sleep and his dreams. He, too, had learned to trust that God would watch out for him, even in his sleep.

CAMELS DON'T FLY

Honk the camel finds a statue of a camel with wings. Now, he is convinced that he can fly, too. Will Honk be the first camel to fly? Find out in the Noah's Park adventure Camels Don't Fly.

STRETCH'S TREASURE HUNT

Stretch the giraffe grew up watching her parents search for the Treasure of Nosy Rock. Imagine what happens when she finds out that the treasure might be buried in Noah's Park. Watch the fur fly as Stretch and her friends look for treasure in Stretch's Treasure Hunt.